# The Crayfish Thief

## Contents

Written by Rachel Mack

Illustrated by Jenny Mountstephen

# Sweet Stream

Sammy and Sarah lived in southeastern Australia. They moved from a big city to the countryside with their mother, father, and grandfather.

There was a stream on their land. And there were woods along the banks of the stream where Sammy and Sarah could play. They loved playing in the stream, but they weren't allowed to go near it by themselves. Their father made them promise never to go to the stream without an adult. So they played in the woods and only went down to the stream when someone could go with them.

"Please, please, please take us down to the stream," they said to their grandfather nearly every day.

Their grandfather loved it down by the stream, too. So he could usually be persuaded to take them whenever they wanted to go.

Grandfather had worked on a steamboat when he was younger, and he loved to sit on the bank and tell Sammy and Sarah stories about all his adventures.

Grandfather had another reason for visiting the stream. He loved to catch crayfish. He trapped them in crayfish pots he kept in the stream.

# No Crayfish for Dinner

It was very exciting for Sammy and Sarah when Grandfather checked his crayfish pots. They knew where each one was, and they would race along, checking each pot, then shouting back to their grandfather if there was a crayfish inside. There nearly always was.

The whole family loved crayfish and they all looked forward to the days when the pots were checked.

One day Sammy and Sarah were sitting by the stream listening to their grandfather tell them yet another of his adventures.

"Well, kids," Grandfather said after he'd finished the story, "I think the pots need checking."

"Race you," shouted Sammy to Sarah, and they jumped up and ran to the first pot.

"It's empty," said Sarah, who got to the pot first.

"Never mind," replied Grandfather, "there's sure to be a crayfish in the next one."

"This one's empty, too!" they heard Sammy shout from the next pot.

"Oh, no," said Sarah, "only one to go!"

Sarah and Sammy raced to the last pot. It was in a deep pool under a tree. At first they had trouble finding it.

"I can see it!" exclaimed Sarah.

"Me, too," said Sammy, "and it's…"

"Empty!" they finished together.

"How strange," said Grandfather. "Well, no crayfish for dinner tonight. We'd better get home and let your mother know. Never mind, I'm sure there'll be some in the pots tomorrow."

# A Crayfish Thief!

The next day was hot and sunny and the children begged their grandfather to take them swimming in the stream. As usual, he was happy to go with them. They could check the crayfish pots at the same time.

The water felt so good that Sammy and Sarah spent most of the day splashing about. Late in the afternoon, Grandfather suggested they check the pots.

"Do you think there might be something in them today?"asked Sammy.

"I think so," answered Grandfather. "The pots have never been empty for two days in a row before! I'm sure we'll be in luck today."

The children raced ahead of their grandfather, eager to see how many crayfish would be in the pots today.

Sammy was the first to reach the pots. He peered down into the first pot.

"Empty," he said sadly.

They walked to the next pot.

"Empty again!" said Sarah, looking down through the clear water into the pot.

"Come on, we still have to check the third pot. It's bound to have a crayfish in it!" said Grandfather cheerfully.

They ran to the last pot, but like it was yesterday, it was empty.

"What's going on, Grandfather?" asked Sammy. "Someone must be stealing our crayfish before we can get to them!"

"I think you're right," said Grandfather. "We'd better go home and talk to your mother and father about this."

# The Trap Is Set

When they got home, Grandfather explained the situation to Sammy and Sarah's parents.

"That's terrible!" exclaimed their mother. "Do you really think someone's stealing our crayfish? Maybe there just aren't many of them out there at the moment."

"But the pots have never been empty for two days in a row before. Something's not right," replied Grandfather. "I wouldn't like to think someone was stealing them. Why don't we set a trap? We could put a crayfish in one of the pots. If it's not there the next day, we'll know we have a crayfish thief on our hands."

"That's a great idea," said their father. "I'll go and buy a crayfish now. It's the only way to know for certain if someone is stealing them."

When Sammy and Sarah's father got back with the crayfish, they all went to the stream and watched Grandfather put it into the third pot in the deepest water.

"It'll be difficult to get that out," said Grandfather smugly. "If there is a thief at all," he added.

It was a long night for Sammy and Sarah. They were both up early, but it was mid-morning by the time everyone else was ready.

When they finally reached the pot, it was empty!

"Now we know," said Grandfather. "Someone is definitely stealing our crayfish."

"This is a real mystery," said Sarah. "Who would do that?"

"I don't know," said their father, "but I've got a plan."

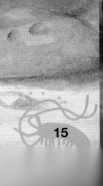

# Stakeout

When they got back to the house, their father explained his idea.

"We'll set a trap with another crayfish, but this time we'll watch from nearby to see who comes to take it," he said.

"Awesome!" shouted Sammy and Sarah together. "A night by the stream!"

"I don't think you two need to go," said their mother. "It's a school night."

"Oh, please, please, can we Dad?" they both begged, turning to their father.

"Your mother's right. If you're both set on coming, we'll have to leave it until next weekend," he said firmly. "You can't be up late during the week."

Sarah and Sammy knew they would have to wait.

It was a long, long week and the children couldn't stop talking about the crayfish thief.

"Maybe it's a runaway kid who's living in the woods and only has crayfish to eat," suggested Sarah.

"Or an escaped prisoner," whispered Sammy.

"I guess we'll just have to wait until Friday to find out," Sarah sighed.

At last, Friday came. Sammy and Sarah's father had collected everything they would need, including another crayfish for the pot.

"Good luck," said their mother as they set off for the stream, carrying biscuits, fruit, drink bottles, and as many warm clothes as they could stuff into their backpacks. "I wish I was going with you instead of going to work this weekend."

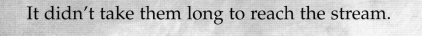

It didn't take them long to reach the stream.

"Let's put the crayfish in this pot," said Grandfather. So their father dropped the crayfish neatly into the pot and they all settled down behind some bushes to watch for the thief.

After what seemed like hours, they heard a rustling in the bushes. They all peered out into the darkness.

"Stay here," whispered their father, and he got up and crept over to the riverbank. Sarah and Sammy moved closer to their grandfather.

"Hold it right there!" Dad suddenly shouted, and he flashed his light right into the face of a small shaggy dog. The dog and their father were both surprised!

"I don't think that's our thief," said Grandfather as the dog ran off.

They all laughed hard. Once he had gotten over the fright, their father laughed as hard as the rest of them.

They had some crackers and some hot chocolate. Time was going by very slowly. Suddenly Sammy and Sarah felt a tugging at their shirt sleeves. Their father was waking them up.

"Oh no, did we fall asleep?" asked Sarah sleepily.

"Did you catch the thief?" asked Sammy.

"No, the thief didn't come," said their father.

"I'll just check the pot to make sure," said Sammy, and he ran down to the stream.

"It's empty!" he shouted.

"It can't be empty!" exclaimed their father, coming to check. "We've been here the whole time. I didn't hear a single thing other than the dog."

Grandfather nodded wisely. "It looks like we're dealing with a very unusual thief," he said.

# Catching a Thief

They spent all the next day making sure that everything would go according to their father's new plan.

This time they chose the second pot. It was in the stream right under the branch of a big tree.

Between them, they made a wall of branches and rocks around the pot, leaving a gap so the thief could still get in. Then they rigged up an old grate from a fireplace just above the surface of the stream.

"Now, I'll lower the grate to catch the thief," Grandfather explained.

When everything was ready, they took their positions. Grandfather waited on the bank. At a signal from their father, he would lower the grate and trap the thief.

Sammy and Sarah thought their father had the best position. He was lying on the overhanging branch looking down into the stream. If he saw anything, he would signal Grandfather. Sammy and Sarah were helping their father watch, but they had to do it from the bank.

They got settled just as the sun began to set.

As soon as the sun went down, Sammy and Sarah spotted a dark shape swimming rapidly over to the crayfish pot. They looked over at Grandfather and frantically waved to give him the signal. He quickly lowered the grate.

They'd done it! They had trapped the thief! Their father climbed down from the tree and they all crowded along the bank, trying to get a better look at what they had caught.

"It's a duck," said Sammy finally.

"It can't be," said Sarah, peering into the dark water. "Ducks don't swim underwater, do they?"

"Is it a beaver?" asked their father uncertainly.

"It's a platypus!" shouted Grandfather. "I haven't seen one of those in years."

"A what-y-pus?" asked Sammy and Sarah together.

"A platypus!" said their father. "I'd forgotten that they live in this area. They're very shy. You don't see them often at all. But they love crayfish – can't get enough of the stuff."

"Dad, we need a flashlight," said Sarah.

Their father ran to get his flashlight. With the light shining on the water, Sammy and Sarah could see the strangest-looking animal. It had a body about the size of a cat, a tail like a beaver, and a snout like a duck's bill.

The platypus swam around and around under the water, in the trap. Every minute or two it came to the surface to breathe.

"We don't want to frighten the poor thing to death," said their father eventually. "We'd better lift the grate and let it go."

He walked over to the rope and pulled the grate up slowly. The platypus went straight through the gap and swam off as fast as it could.

"Well, well, we finally solved the mystery of the crayfish thief," said Grandfather. "Now all we need to do is figure out how we can get it to share!"